Acting Edition

Summer, 1976

by David Auburn

No one shall make any changes in this title(s) for the purpose of production. No part of this book may be reproduced, stored in a retrieval system, scanned, uploaded, or transmitted in any form, by any means, now known or yet to be invented, including mechanical, electronic, digital, photocopying, recording, videotaping, or otherwise, without the prior written permission of the publisher. No one shall share this title(s), or any part of this title(s), through any social media or file hosting websites.

For all inquiries regarding motion picture, television, online/digital and other media rights, please contact Concord Theatricals Corp.

MUSIC AND THIRD-PARTY MATERIALS USE NOTE

Licensees are solely responsible for obtaining formal written permission from copyright owners to use copyrighted music and/or other copyrighted third-party materials (e.g. artworks, logos) in the performance of this play and are strongly cautioned to do so. If no such permission is obtained by the licensee, then the licensee must use only original music and materials that the licensee owns and controls. Licensees are solely responsible and liable for clearances of all third-party copyrighted materials, including without limitation music, and shall indemnify the copyright owners of the play(s) and their licensing agent, Concord Theatricals Corp., against any costs, expenses, losses and liabilities arising from the use of such copyrighted third-party materials by licensees. For music, please contact the appropriate music licensing authority in your territory for the rights to any incidental music.

IMPORTANT BILLING AND CREDIT REQUIREMENTS

If you have obtained performance rights to this title, please refer to your licensing agreement for important billing and credit requirements.

SUMMER, 1976 was originally commissioned by the Manhattan Theatre Club (Lynne Meadow, Artistic Director; Barry Grove, Executive Producer) with funds provided by Bank of America, and received its world premiere there on April 25, 2023. The performance was directed by Daniel Sullivan, with scenic design by John Lee Beatty, costume design by Linda Cho, lighting design by Japhy Weideman, sound design by Jill BC Du Boff, projection design by Hana S. Kim, and original music by Greg Pliska. The Production Stage Manager was James FitzSimmons. The cast was as follows:

DIANA . . . . Laura Linney
ALICE . . . . Jessica Hecht

CHARACTERS

DIANA
ALICE

1.

DIANA. We became friends, as you often do, through our children.

I didn't like her child, actually. A little girl, Holly – I hate the name Holly – her nose was always running, her mother constantly calling her over and wiping it for her whenever she came over to play with my daughter, Gretchen.

The girls would ask to use my studio for art projects. My art studio was *strictly off limits*, which Gretchen knew, so that meant Holly put her up to it: She'd certainly calculated that I wouldn't want to look unkind and controlling in front of my friend, her mother – small children are devious that way – that I'd be forced to say Of course, kids! Run amuck in my studio. And while you're at it never mind your own colored pencils and Big Chief pads, use the rapidographs that I bought in art school with the proceeds from my grandmother's savings bond! And the Strathmore Bristol Board too!

But I showed them – NO, I'd say very firmly, you may *not* use my studio, that is where I *work*, it's not a place for play, Gretchen you *know* that and Holly you'll find a box of tissues in the bathroom, why don't you carry it *with* you?

And now leave the mommys alone, we're talking. Go outside.

And they'd slink off appropriately cowed. And Alice and I would be alone to talk and sometimes share a joint she'd brought.

Parents who can't or won't control their kids aren't upset when you do it for them. They're grateful and ashamed.

ALICE. The pot came from Merle, a student who was painting our house at the time.

My husband Doug taught at Ohio State and we had a nice little house. Merle was one of his students who needed money so we hired him that summer. Despite being pretty stoned most of the time he did a good job, but he was slow.

We'd been in Columbus for three years and there were a bunch of young faculty parents with small children on tight budgets so we started this thing, it was a babysitting co-op.

Really Doug started it. He's an economist – he worked it all out, he had a rubber stamp made and he stamped out these coupons – although he called them "shares" – and distributed them to all the parents in the group.

The idea was you could trade these "shares" for babysitting, an hour or two hours or whatever at a time. That way no one had to pay cash for child care, you could just exchange these papers back and forth and around, like if you went out Wednesday night you'd spend two or three shares but you'd get them back when you sat for somebody else on Friday, and it would all work out in perpetuity somehow; Doug had proved it mathematically.

Sure, whatever.

We didn't go out that much. I was bored that summer. Doug was working and I mostly just hung around the house supervising Merle, tanning, reading paperback novels and watching Holly splash around in her little inflatable pool.

One afternoon another woman in the co-op called me up. A professor in the Art Department. She had a project to finish and she needed sitting for her daughter, Gretchen. I told her sure, bring Gretchen over.

Both girls were about five and they played all afternoon. When she came to pick Gretchen up she tried to give me three shares for the three hours but I was like come on, this wasn't *sitting*, the kids were *playing*, they were entertaining each other. I benefitted too, I got to read *Shōgun*.

She was kind of thrown by that and annoyed, like, "But isn't there a system?" She seemed kind of uptight.

I was like, if you want to give me the shares, OK, but I really don't care, it's all sort of bullshit anyway, right? I mean, Doug just *made* these with his rubber stamp, they don't actually have *value*.

She said of course they have value because we *assign* them value, like any currency or monetary instrument.

She said "monetary instrument."

I really didn't want to get into a whole philosophical debate about it and also I sort of immediately hated her so I took the shares and she took her kid home.

The problem was Holly and Gretchen had hit it off, and soon they wanted to spend every afternoon together.

DIANA. Of course I could tell she didn't like me, this sleepy-eyed little hippie with her shorts and her coconut oil and her sun-bleached paperback copy of James Clavell's depressingly middlebrow novel *Shōgun*, which she was toting around proudly like it was *The Brothers Karamazov*.

There is no one more condescending and judgmental than a self-imagined "free spirit" smugly encountering a "square," but let me tell you I knew exactly what she was up to on I'd say it was about the third afternoon she brought her daughter over, and I had politely offered her an iced tea – it was a very hot afternoon – as we sat on my screened-in porch watching the girls in the yard, and she said No thanks and opened up her little macramé handbag and lit up a joint instead!

When she offered it to me I knew she was expecting a shocked stammering and fluttering of hands and an opportunity to feel superior so I showed her: I took the biggest deepest hit I could and held it for an age and blew it out and didn't hand the joint back but took another *massive*, really industrial-vacuum suck before demurely relinquishing it.

The look on her face!

ALICE. Yeah, she fucking bogarted it for like five minutes, and I was like, come on lady, I only took it out because it was the only way I could imagine getting through the next ten minutes before I could make an excuse and leave. I'd already had to look at her art since four or five of her, like, pieces were scattered around on the porch – she said she worked out there sometimes – and get a mini-lecture about each one, except strike the "mini" part.

They *were* good.

I pointed out one I particularly liked.

DIANA. It's not finished.

ALICE. I still like it.

DIANA. *None* of them are.

ALICE. Why not?

DIANA. That's just how it is.

ALICE. Okay.

They weren't just one thing, one medium: they were paintings with ink drawing and things scratched away or glued on, you know, a variety of techniques in each one, sort of like Paul Klee, who I'd always liked, but by an American and a woman.

DIANA. She muttered something about Paul Klee as we talked about my work and the pot clicked in, and I was surprised.

Sorry – I was, first, briefly but keenly *chagrined*: I was no longer influenced by Klee *at all*, it was something I had worked very hard to get *away* from, actually, I'd sweat *blood* to expunge the embarrassingly jejune infatuation I'd had with his work as an art student.

But I was surprised that she knew him.

ALICE. We got hungry of course and were digging through her fridge when the kids came in for popsicles. She gave them some neon-colored store-bought ones from the freezer which Holly was *ecstatic* about since I only made the homemade orange juice kind which admittedly were kind of gross but you know, they were cheap; and the kids went back outside, and we tucked into her leftovers which were *incredible*: it turned out she was a *serious* cook, we ate cassoulet out of a Tupperware, cold (microwaves were still rare then) – God, I can still remember how fucking delicious it was, sitting on her kitchen floor stoned on a summer afternoon.

After that, yeah, we were friends.

2.

DIANA. Who was Gretchen's father? A boy I had met in art school, and gotten pregnant by on our second date – he took me to see *Beneath the Planet of the Apes*, which disheartened me, but not enough to overcome the sheer and as it turned out fleeting animal lust I felt for that lush-lipped, golden-haired, deeply not-bright glass-blower.

Smells are powerful and the erotic for me remains deeply bound up with the chemical tang of the art supplies that were always close at hand during those intense, formative sexual experiences. Oil paint; the photographic developer in the darkrooms where so many humid couplings took place; varnishes and patinas; blown-glass pigments...

But back to the boy. Two dates was enough; after that – and a third afternoon's farewell fuck when I went by his place to retrieve the case containing the diaphragm I had neglected, in a moment of madness, to use during date number two – I avoided him on campus and ignored his phone calls and eventually he got the message – he was just too dull, the poor thing.

He dropped out of school the next semester. I've no idea where he wound up.

Sometimes when I stumble onto one of those touring craft fairs they erect next to farmers markets in the summertime – you know, the ones with the candles and the leather notebook covers and the table lamps made of old typewriter parts or God knows what aesthetic atrocity – if I spot a hand-blown glass display tended by a man the right age (beard, greying ponytail, thick middle) I'll think: This could, in theory, be the father of my daughter.

Not that I care all that much.

ALICE. A couple times I wondered about Gretchen's father but never asked, figuring bad divorce, but who knows, maybe death? Since she never brought it up? At all? 'Til one day – this was after we'd been hanging out for a couple weeks maybe – she told me her art school story.

And I was kind of surprised. It was hard to square. I should describe her house so you understand. It was incredibly orderly, and incredibly nice, with all this very carefully chosen midcentury modern furniture that she knew the history of and would describe for you in *great detail* – don't get me wrong: it was really interesting, everything she said was interesting, she really knew a lot, like, *everything* about twentieth century art and design. You could see how she must have been a really good teacher.

And I mentioned her food – her kitchen was the same as the rest of the house: immaculate, and thought-out: spice jars alphabetized, copper pots hanging just so in order of size, that kind of thing.

So I couldn't quite square it. This meticulous, very controlled person. And just having a baby like that, like, kind of accidentally and randomly and what-the-hell.

And then, all the fancy gourmet food, but junky store-bought popsicles. Or seeming so uptight, but *really* enthusiastic about my grass.

So it made me think – I mean, this is obvious now but it seemed like a big revelation at the time, I was young – that people aren't just one thing.

And it made me kind of question myself.

DIANA. She thought of herself as a "free spirit" but she was in the most conventional of marriages: she wasn't working, she was essentially living like a 1950s housewife.

She just *thought* she was unconventional because her house was messy. I mean that's all it was really.

When I went over there – we alternated afternoons – I was horrified. It wasn't just the clutter, or the makeshift college-apartment furniture, the brick-and-plank bookshelves, the art exhibition posters *in no frames – just tacked up directly to the wall!* It was the whole bullshit bead-curtain-in-the-doorway gestalt of the place. The house *badly* needed a paint job and rather than hiring professionals it was being done by a graduate student, *by himself*: one shambolic goon with a roller on a rickety ladder. It was taking all summer! A job that could have been done in four days by professionals!

ALICE. We couldn't *afford* professionals!

And yeah we had shitty furniture but we'd put all our money into the house and Doug was always working – he was up for tenure the next spring and this summer was make-or-break, he was finishing three different articles and figured he had to get at least two published before the tenure committee met if he was going to have a shot; we didn't have time to, like, decorate.

She said, don't *decorate*. Just buy *one good piece*.

I said I don't know what that means!

DIANA. I will show you what it means.

ALICE. So we drove to Cleveland. To a place she knew, a gigantic dusty auction house crammed with furniture from estate sales, defunct Great Lakes resorts, bankrupt corporations, that kind of thing.

DIANA. I knew the owners, a pair of brothers, Arthur and George.

ALICE. And not just furniture. Chandeliers, carpets, mantelpieces, strips of moulding, and those wood panel wall things...

DIANA. *Wainscotting.*

ALICE. ...Whole *ceilings* that had been removed from fancy houses somehow. I'd never seen anything like it! She bargained for me when I saw what I wanted: a desk.

DIANA. I said You don't want a desk, Alice, you want something to pull a room together. Your living room sofa is a hide-a-bed, for God's sake, replace that!

ALICE. But I liked this desk.

DIANA. It *was* interesting. A 1930s tubular steel Bauhaus design, a bit banged up but the real thing; not cheap.

ALICE. No way could I afford it.

DIANA. I bought it for her.

ALICE. No WAY am I gonna let you do that, are you kidding me?

DIANA. She objected but I could see how badly she wanted it.

ALICE. I didn't even know what I'd do with it!

I just felt sure if it was in my house and I was sitting at it I'd do...*something*.

But still, she was *not* going to just buy it for me, that is just crazy! I don't even know why you'd *want* to –

DIANA. Pipe down and let me bargain.

I haggled with Arthur and George and got them down to a reasonable number.

We put the desk in the back of her station wagon; the hatch wouldn't close all the way but we secured it with twine and drove the two hours back to Columbus like that.

ALICE. This desk cost *three hundred dollars*. In 1976 that seemed like a fortune. By comparison we were paying Merle 175 dollars to paint the house and that was a stretch for us. It was bananas. I told her I'd pay her back. I *insisted* on it. She sort of shrugged, waved it off.

(**DIANA** *does this.*)

I didn't know what that meant. Was it "Shut up about it, it's done"? Or was it I *could* pay her back – even though I didn't know how I'd possibly do that. I was kind of too embarrassed to pursue it. I figured – I rationalized it really – that she must have family money.

DIANA. I did have family money.

ALICE. But still, Jesus! A three hundred dollar antique desk! Doug worked on two filing cabinets and a door.

DIANA. We set up the desk in a corner of her living room.

The room looked much worse with the desk in it. Everything else was so outclassed.

Oh well. I'd tried.

Then it was time to fetch our respective daughters. We'd spent the whole day together.

3.

ALICE. Now it's I think a couple weeks later.

Doug wanted to go to this lecture on campus by some visiting big-wig economist. Apparently he'd told me about it months earlier but I'd forgotten because why wouldn't I?

But it turned out there would be a private dinner party after and wives were "expected," for whatever reason; everybody was supposed to get dressed up and go and kiss this guy's ass, sure, fine. I didn't mind these events. I liked going out, even if the lecture itself would be a snore.

But we didn't have any shares left, you know, the sitting coupons. I'd spent *seven* on the trip to Cleveland, yikes, and I hadn't been taking any from Diana, or her from me – we'd sort of forgotten about using them.

All right, so we're just gonna have to pay a sitter, I said.

And Doug was like, *cash*?

Yeah, cash.

But that would negate the whole point of the *system*. He went to a lot of trouble to set up that system. It's a *cashless, self-sustaining system*!

I was like, well, but it's not. I mean it's not sustaining itself, is it?

It *would*, if we weren't spending more than we were taking in.

Sorry, that was Doug. This is getting confusing. She'll do Doug from here on, OK?

DIANA. *(As Doug.)* It *would*, if we weren't spending more than we were taking in.

ALICE. All right, Doug, so what do people do in the real world when they're spending more than they take in? They borrow, right? Can't we just get some more shares somehow?

DIANA. *(As Doug.)* Alice, they go *bankrupt*.

And this *is* the real world! Look, the whole, the fundamental problem is you're thinking of the co-op as an *abstraction*, one that's only *modeling* real-world behavior, instead of a *functioning monetary system* designed to *constrain* and *optimize* that behavior!

ALICE. Oh blah blah fucking blah – this is all happening when we're trying to get dressed for the party and it annoys the *shit* out of me the way he tries to turn everything into a fucking seminar, I'm not one of his goddamn students.

While he was in the bathroom I went to his study and got his rubber stamp and just *made* three new shares, bam bam bam.

Doug! Honey! Good news, whew! I was wrong, I've got a couple shares left after all, we're good for tonight!

So we went to the thing, and actually apart from the lecture we had a decent time.

DIANA. Her husband seemed unbearably drab, honestly, but I'd only met him once – the afternoon we brought in the desk and he stared at it with a baffled, resigned look on his face before retreating back into his study – but she seemed content with him and no outsider can understand what makes another person's marriage tick.

The month of July I recall as a sort of idyll. Me, and Alice, and Holly, and Gretchen, together most days, finding things to do in Columbus. A museum, a movie, the *excellent* zoo, a dairy outside of town that made their own ice cream.

There were endless commemorations with band concerts and fireworks that bicentennial summer and Alice and I went to several with the girls. Doug, who I was told hated fireworks, usually stayed home. I *adore* fireworks.

I began to like Holly much more. Her nose stopped running. I'd suggested to Alice she might have allergies and Alice got her checked out and I was right, and she put her on allergy shots and the transformation was wonderful to behold. A bright and ebullient child had been hiding behind all that snot.

And I liked Holly's mother. She knew how to stand up for herself. She knew how to stand up to *me*. One day we were lying out by the public pool with our books while the girls splashed around and I guess I'd made one too many snide remarks about her choice of reading material – it was *Coma* by Robin Cook now that she was done with *Shōgun*, a step down if that was possible, and she rounded right on me:

ALICE. You're a snob, Diana.

DIANA. I am not!

ALICE. It's OK, I don't mind and you can't help it anyway, but if I want to read crap during the summertime I'm going to do it. All the stuff I know you think I should be reading, the stuff I see on your bookshelves, Henry James and Virginia Woolf and Thomas Hardy and *Middlemarch*, I've read them too, you know. I read all that shit in college and grad school. I'm aware *Middlemarch* is "better" than *Coma*. You don't have to educate me on that score. It's a controversial stance you're taking but yeah, when it comes to narrative fiction George Eliot *does* have a slight edge over Robin Cook. OK? Now can you please shut the fuck up and let me finish reading *Coma* in peace because there's a James Michener book about Hawaii I'm dying to get to next.

DIANA. I didn't know she'd gone to graduate school.

ALICE. I did a year at the University of Iowa. Then I dropped out.

DIANA. Why?

ALICE. I married Doug. Got pregnant with Holly. And Doug got the job in Columbus.

DIANA. Why didn't you continue on at Ohio State? I wanted to ask, but sensed I shouldn't, so I left it there.

Our growing intimacy was cemented one afternoon the day after a fireworks display – it might have been the big one on the fourth of July, actually – when I thought I was going to die.

I'm not trying to be melodramatic. I'm trying to be accurate to my sense of things at the time.

I'd always suffered from migraines. "Suffered" is both the conventional term and *le mot juste*; the best description I can give you of the experience is, it's as if someone were trying very hard but failing to extract your eyeballs through a hole drilled in the back of your skull.

The only thing worse than a migraine is a migraine when you have a small child to look after.

You cannot function.

In the past if I was lucky and it hit after dinnertime I could put Gretchen in front of the television – PBS only darling, you know the rules, promise me – and crawl into bed with an icepack on my face and a vomit bucket on the floor – sleep would be impossible but with luck *please, please Christ please* by dawn the demonic surgeon will have set down his tools and I could stagger out, find Gretchen drowsy and stirring on the couch, and pretend Mommy just had a little cold, it's much better now, should we make blueberry pancakes? Even as the thought of them made me retch and gag.

But this time it came a little after noon. You know when it's coming. There's no pain at first. Colors have a nervous vibrancy and you feel this strangely giddy dread. Nothing to be done. Here it comes. Batten down the hatches.

I called Alice. Please come over, *now*. I'm going to need you.

ALICE. Doug was working, as usual. I left Holly at home with him. The way Diana's voice sounded scared me. I hadn't known her long but I'd never heard her voice sound like that.

I found her dry-heaving in her bathroom, and pressing her face against the tile for the coolness, and crying.

Somehow I got her into her bedroom. She wanted the place sealed up, no light, and the air on full blast even though she was shivering. I just did what she said. I was kind of freaked out. I didn't know anything about migraines and thought I should probably take her to a hospital but she begged me to just do what she asked, so I did.

I stayed the rest of the afternoon, and all night, and the next morning. I kept Gretchen calm, let her watch all the crap TV her mother usually forbid (I think *Charlie's Angels* was on), made her supper. Emptied her mom's puke bucket and brought her wet washcloths I chilled in the freezer. She finally came out of it around two PM the next afternoon.

DIANA. As much as the giddiness that precedes them, there's a species of joy *following* the migraine that's equally strange.

Because it's not simple joy at the release from pain – the joy you'd expect.

It's a different feeling.

An awareness of how much pleasure there is to be taken in the world. That you only possess in such intensity *because* you've endured the hateful thing. And somehow, *gratitude* to the hateful thing for making the awareness possible.

The cup of coffee she made for me when it was finally over and I came out into my kitchen was the most delicious thing I'd ever tasted.

ALICE. Doug was pissed he lost a day of work. Well, tough.

4.

ALICE. The next thing to tell you about is when I started to get the distinct impression that Merle was into me.

Look, I'm not super-vain, I never have been, I wasn't going around always thinking guys were trying to get into my pants, but I was reasonably cute back then and it was summer and I was laying out in a bikini a lot or at least a bikini top, and Doug was up in his office all the time and Merle took frequent breaks.

Mustache, jean shorts, sun visor, John Lennon glasses, Jimmy Connors bowl haircut, Jesus sandals, Muppets T-shirt. Not bad. Not great by today's standards, but an OK look then.

I couldn't have been more than three or four years older than him. Actually we might have been the same age. But he still spoke to me weirdly formally, calling me by my last name – actually my *married* name which I didn't even use – asking if it was OK if he could go inside and use the bathroom or get a drink of water or whatever.

Keep in mind there was a power dynamic between us because not only were we employing him but my husband was his master's thesis advisor, but it was still ridiculous. I said, Merle, you don't have to ask me every time you want to go inside. Just do whatever you need, OK? And call me Alice.

After that he relaxed a little, and we became kind of friendly, and chatted sometimes, and this was when I'd sometimes buy a joint or two off him, and things were cool.

But then one day he seemed to be going up and down his ladder *a lot*, and finally on about the fourth trip inside in like an hour I said, Jeez, Merle, you're pissing like a racehorse today.

He *froze*, turned *really* red, and his chin trembled, and it looked like he was going to cry!

I was like, *What the hell?*

Oh my God, Merle, I'm so sorry. I didn't mean anything. I don't know why I said that. That's just a stupid phrase my granddad used to use. I don't care how much you piss, I mean pee, I really don't. Or whatever you're doing in there.

He just stammered, like, No, no, no, it's nothing, and shot back up his ladder like a squirrel and didn't come down the rest of the day.

DIANA. Well obviously the frequent trips inside were so that he could walk by and ogle your tits in your bikini top.

ALICE. What? Come on, you're out of your mind.

DIANA. Of course! That's why he was so embarrassed when you called him on it! Don't play *faux naïf*, Alice. You've probably been all flirty, playing the hip hausfrau, sharing his drugs and giving him the eye, don't deny it.

ALICE. I –

DIANA. And don't make me spell out what he was *doing* in there on each of those trips after ogling you in your bikini top either.

ALICE. Now *that* is ridiculous. Not four times in one hour.

DIANA. Maybe not four, no. But unless he has a medical condition I can think of no other solution to the Case of the Peripatetic House Painter.

ALICE. Well now I was worried he really *did* have a medical condition that made him have to pee all the time and I seemed like a huge bitch for making fun of him about it.

I mean, look at it from his point of view – he's working his ass off in the hot sun all summer *seriously ill* –

DIANA. Oh come on, he doesn't have a *medical condition*.

ALICE. – and there's this little spoiled nitwit lounging on a towel *mocking* his condition while he desperately tries to complete the job her husband, who holds his career in his hands, is paying him *a pittance* for – God, I felt like Marie Antoinette or something.

DIANA. If you feel so guilty why don't you just fuck him?

ALICE. Diana!

DIANA. Well why not? I've seen him. He's all right in a goonish sort of way. I've seen the way he paints your house. He's patient and meticulous. That bodes well for sexual competence.

ALICE. Ugh.

DIANA. Why not give it a try?

ALICE. I'm married!

DIANA. Yes?

ALICE. That *means* something to me. Jesus! I don't just go around sleeping with other guys just because I want to.

DIANA. So you do want to. With – what's his name?

ALICE. Merle. No, I don't!

DIANA. You said you did.

ALICE. Not with Merle.

DIANA. But generally?

ALICE. No!

DIANA. Are you sure about that?

ALICE. Will you cut it out? Why are you doing this?

DIANA. I want you to be happy, Alice, that's all, and you're clearly not.

ALICE. Of course I'm happy!

DIANA. Are you?

ALICE. I – Are *you*?

DIANA. No. I'm not. Thank you for asking.

The difference between us is I don't try to fake it.

(**ALICE** *gets up and leaves.*)

She stormed out of my house.

ALICE. God, she really pissed me off.

DIANA. I was surprised. What had I said?

ALICE. I didn't talk to her for a few days.

DIANA. I called. She didn't answer.

ALICE. I just let the phone ring.

DIANA. What had I said?

ALICE. That thing of telling me how I "really" felt, what I "really" wanted, only I was too stupid or naive or whatever to realize it? That especially got to me. Like she was the adult and I was the child. She wasn't older than me. Maybe by a couple years. Like *she* had all the life experience. Why? Because she was alone? She obviously thought she could "improve" me. That stuff with the desk and everything – the desk was immediately buried under mail and magazines and other crap, by the way; I never used it, not even to pay bills, I just sat at the kitchen table. Maybe I'd made a mistake getting so close to her so fast.

DIANA. Eventually she did pick up.

ALICE. Yeah?

DIANA. Look, I have tickets to the Emerson String Quartet at Weigel Hall on Thursday night, they're young but they're supposed to be very good.

ALICE. Great.

DIANA. Do you want to go?

ALICE. I can't. Doug and I have got a thing.

DIANA. Clearly a lie.

Are you lying?

ALICE. You tell me, Diana, you're so perceptive and wise about everything, right?

DIANA. It was like talking to a teenager.

Well, that's too bad. I would have liked to go with you.

ALICE. Yeah, well.

Maybe I was overdoing it. But I still didn't want to see her.

Really awkward pause. She still hadn't hung up.

What?

DIANA. The thing is…

ALICE. What?

DIANA. I still need babysitting.

For the concert. I'm still going to go. I'm not about to waste the tickets.

ALICE. Yeah, uh, sorry, I'm not going to *sit* for you, Diana, I told you, Doug and I –

DIANA. We both know that's not true but nevermind. No, the point is I'm out of shares, I wondered if you could loan me some?

ALICE. No. I'm out too.

DIANA. Why do we both always seem to be out?

ALICE. 'Cause Doug's system is stupid.

DIANA. Well, you and I haven't been making use of the scrip, that probably warped things a bit, you can't blame poor Doug for that.

ALICE. Uh huh.

Look, I guess I can maybe get you some more shares.

DIANA. No, you don't have to do that, I'll find a local high school girl and pay cash.

ALICE. No, it's OK. I can get you some, it's no problem.

DIANA. Don't do anything "illegal."

ALICE. It's fine. I'll leave them in an envelope on our front porch, you can pick them up whenever.

DIANA. Well, thank you.

ALICE. Sure. Okay then.

DIANA. Okay.

ALICE. It was definitely uncomfortable. I don't know. I don't think it was my fault.

DIANA. Something had happened. Some corner turned in the friendship. Some ground lost. How much?

ALICE. Still, I'd promised her the shares so after I hung up I went to Doug's study and got his stamp and made a bunch for Diana. I made a bunch of extra ones for myself too in case I needed some sometime.

When Doug suddenly *burst* into his office, scaring the *shit* out of me, I barely had time to jam the stamp into the back pocket of my shorts.

Hi! Just getting an envelope!

He looked really upset. He said he needed to talk to me.

DIANA. In the end I couldn't find a sitter so I took Gretchen to the concert.

That night the very charismatic young string quartet was playing Shostakovich Eight, that most harrowing, gutting cry of bitterness and pain.

Shostakovich wrote the piece, in case you've forgotten, in a spasm of agonized self-loathing for his capitulation to Stalinism, and in physical agony from his encroaching degenerative nerve disease besides.

I tried to explain all this to Gretchen before the performance but somehow it didn't seem to pique her interest much. She hadn't wanted to come in the first place. She'd wanted to stay home and watch *Charlie's Angels*, her "new favorite show."

How did the music affect me?

To my surprise I found myself unmoved, and experienced old Shosty's exquisite and well-earned despair as merely lugubrious, and tiresome, and too easy to succumb to.

I wanted my friend with me, to roll her eyes and make rude comments, and make me giggle behind my program at the solemnity of everyone around us.

I *miss* you –

ALICE. Doug said.

And there were tears in his eyes!

DIANA. *(As Doug.)* I feel like I never see you.

ALICE. Well, you're working so much.

DIANA. *(As Doug.)* I know! I know, I know, I'm not blaming you. It's not your fault. It's me. These fucking papers –

ALICE. The journal articles he was trying to finish so he could get tenure hopefully.

DIANA. *(As Doug.)* – I'm trying to finish them but they just won't *stay finished*, they keep getting away from me, half the time I don't even know what the hell I'm saying with them anymore…

ALICE. It was very unlike Doug to ever express any doubt about his work, that was one area where he was totally confident, arrogant really, he thought he was really a hot shit young academic and his sort of nerdy swagger was something I actually found quite sexy about him when we first met.

Hey, hey, hey, you're gonna get them done. They're gonna be great. You're gonna blow the tenure committee away –

DIANA. *(As Doug.)* Anyway, that's not the point. I don't want to talk about work. It's *me*.

ALICE. You?

DIANA. *(As Doug.)* I mean us. I mean…

ALICE. An eternity here while Doug paused for breath, then made a visible effort to reset and start again:

DIANA. *(As Doug.)* I know you've been alone. I know you're stuck with all the child care. You don't complain, but I know you must be lonely and bored, you must be really frustrated with me, and –

ALICE. I haven't been lonely.

DIANA. *(As Doug.)* Yeah, I know, your friend, the art adjunct woman, that's great but what I'm saying is, I'm sorry the summer's been such a drag. Let's just go away, OK? Let's go away as a family for a couple days.

ALICE. Wait, *adjunct*? I thought she was a professor.

DIANA. *(As Doug.)* Who?

ALICE. Diana. My friend.

DIANA. *(As Doug.)* Are we talking about the same person? The one who gave you that weird desk?

ALICE. Yes.

DIANA. *(As Doug.)* No, no, I don't think so. I think she's just part-time.

ALICE. No, she's in Fine Arts.

DIANA. *(As Doug.)* No. She teaches continuing ed or something like that, she's not in the Department.

ALICE. Oh.

DIANA. *(As Doug.)* Anyway, look, let's leave tomorrow.

We'll drive up to Sandusky and find an inexpensive motel on the Lake and swim and... Alice?

ALICE. What?

DIANA. *(As Doug.)* Are you listening? What do you say?

ALICE. Sorry. I – yes. Of course. Of course, Doug. Yes.

He kissed me.

I was really touched.

Except my shorts were ruined – the ink on the rubber stamp bled through the pocket and wouldn't come out.

Doug went to tell Holly about the trip.

DIANA. Let's surprise Holly! I said, and bundled Gretchen into the car the next morning around ten AM and drove over to their house.

The envelope with the co-op shares was on the porch where she said it would be, but the house was empty and their car was gone.

Lanky Merle was mixing paint in the driveway. He told me Alice, Doug and Holly had gone on a little vacation, he wasn't sure how long they'd be away.

Alice hadn't said anything about a vacation to me.

Gretchen burst into tears on hearing her friend was gone. I think she misunderstood the circumstances. "It's only for a few days, darling," I told her, although I didn't know that for sure.

It was already a fiercely hot morning and she'd been looking forward to sharing Holly's inflatable wading pool. Not wanting to disappoint her further, or risk a squall, I asked the laconic Merle if I could let Gretchen use it for a bit. He shrugged, seemingly confused as to why I'd bothered to ask his permission for anything, which to be honest I was too, and soon Gretchen was splashing away contentedly while I sat sweaty and torpid in a lawn chair, watching the loose-limbed and meticulous Merle dipping and stroking with his paint brush – he was on to the fine work on the trimmings now – atop the ladder.

I must have dozed off.

When I awoke my throat was on fire with thirst so I went inside to get something to drink. There was no sign of Merle – he must have been on one of his famous breaks.

I was standing at the kitchen sink waiting for the water to run cold when I felt calloused hands on my shoulders and smelled the cool astringent tang of latex all-weather house paint.

I knew immediately what was happening; there was no surprise, no shock as one of the hands moved to a breast, the other to my waist, first, then lower to lift the hem of the thin sun-dress I'd worn that day, by which time I was already ankling out of my underwear. All this without turning around, mind you. I gripped the edge of the sink, and – Oh Christ, what was I *doing*? Had I actually left a six-year-old child alone in a swimming pool while I was inside getting fucked in Alice's kitchen by Merle the fucking house painter? But it was just a splash pool, you couldn't drown in six inches of water, could you? *Of course you could!* This is not good parenting, I told myself, even as I succumbed to a crashing tsunami of lust.

It was then that I heard Gretchen begin to scream.

ALICE. We had a nice couple days up in Sandusky. I don't know what else to say about it, really, it was just nice. Good weather, cheap motel but clean, Mom & Pop. Holly and Doug built sandcastles on the beach for hours, we ate take-out hamburgers in the room at night and watched TV all together. Doug and I even made love once, very quietly, under the covers late at night in the motel room, after Holly was fast asleep on the fold-out cot the motel provided. It was just nice.

DIANA. She'd been stung by a wasp.

I lurched out of the lawn chair, instantly awake, my child's cries dissolving the sex-dream like smoke.

In the kitchen, an ice cube on the back of her knee where the sting was and an orange juice popsicle from the recesses of Alice's freezer eventually stilled the sobs.

Merle, who'd emerged stoned from somewhere, looked on stupidly, shuffling in his sandals, a confused, paint-splattered, unhelpful presence. I noticed his toenails. They were long and yellowish. Here was the object of my erotic reverie. Ludicrous. Pathetic. I felt a crunch of self-loathing and self-pity in my guts.

ALICE. *(As Gretchen.)* Why are you crying?

DIANA. I'm not, Gretchen. Don't be silly.

ALICE. When we got back, the house was finished. Trim, everything. Merle had done a *great* job. It looked like a million bucks! I was really impressed.

Doug said we should have a little party, like an end-of-the-summer thing to celebrate and show off the "new" house before the fall quarter got underway. Doug was like a different person after that little vacation. I guess he really needed it.

We decided on a Friday night for the party. I started to make some calls to invite people.

DIANA. She called me. It was the first time we'd spoken since she went away. I said I'd be very glad to come, thank you.

Is there anything I can bring?

ALICE. No, no, just bring yourself.

DIANA. OK. Gretchen can't wait to see Holly, she's missed her.

ALICE. Oh, no, uh, it's not a kid's thing. Doug wants to have like a proper grown-up dinner party thing.

DIANA. Oh. I see.

ALICE. But we can figure out another time to get the kids together, yeah?

DIANA. Good, yes.

ALICE. Holly's missed Gretchen too.

DIANA. You're sure it's all right? If it's all couples the last thing I want is to be in the way.

ALICE. You won't be "in the way," don't be ridiculous. We'd love to have you.

(Beat.)

DIANA. Where did you go? We happened to stop by the house, we were driving by, you weren't there…

ALICE. Oh, we just had a chance to get away for a few days, so we grabbed it. Family time, you know.

DIANA. That's lovely.

ALICE. Yeah, it was really nice.

DIANA. A pause here, while I waited for her to say something like What's going on with you? Or What have you been up to?

ALICE. So – see you Friday, yeah? Around seven.

DIANA. Seven o'clock. See you Friday.

ALICE. Was she glad I had called? I couldn't tell.

DIANA. Our rift was not healed exactly, but it was a gesture, one I appreciated.

ALICE. Did she even want to come at all? I figured, whatever, I'd see her at the party Friday and we'd figure it out probably.

DIANA. And I did see her Friday.

But there was no party.

5.

ALICE. I started worrying about what to make to eat. I'd been given a *Joy of Cooking* and a Julia Child by my mother when I got married but as I might have mentioned I was not a great cook so I needed to pick something simple but still impressive hopefully. I was working on that when Doug came into the kitchen. He had a kind of strange look on his face.

DIANA. *(As Doug.)* I just talked to Nathan Robinoff.

ALICE. Oh great. Are they coming?

DIANA. *(As Doug.)* He and Maria are having a little trouble getting sitting.

ALICE. The Robinoffs were in the co-op Doug set up, a lot of his departmental colleagues were.

Oh, well, hopefully they can find something.

DIANA. *(As Doug.)* I'm sure they will. But it was the *reason* they were having trouble.

ALICE. What?

DIANA. *(As Doug.)* They asked a couple of other people in the co-op...

ALICE. Yeah?

DIANA. *(As Doug.)* None of them wanted to sit.

ALICE. Must be a busy night. Maybe there's other parties.

DIANA. *(As Doug.)* No, they *could* sit, but nobody *wanted* to. Because they all have plenty of shares. They have too many already.

ALICE. Oh, well, maybe they can just pay somebody.

DIANA. *(As Doug.)* I'm sure they can. But it's just...

ALICE. He went away looking really troubled.

I started to have a sick feeling in my stomach but I tried to focus on the menu issue. I decided I'd make a lasagna, I figured I could handle that, and make a big salad and have lots of bread in case it turned out crap. I was heading out to the grocery when Doug came in again.

DIANA. *(As Doug.)* I don't get it. I called a bunch of other co-op members and *everyone's* in surplus. There's some kind of glut in shares. Nobody wants more. Some people are having to spend three or four shares to get an hour's sitting instead of one.

ALICE. Oh that's too bad. I'm sure it'll sort itself out.

DIANA. *(As Doug.)* No, it won't. Do you understand what this is?

ALICE. No.

DIANA. *(As Doug.)* It's *inflation.*

ALICE. Gosh.

DIANA. *(As Doug.)* I don't understand how this is possible. I worked it out very carefully. I can see how the system could go into recession but not how it could be *inflationary,* the number of shares is *fixed,* there's no central bank minting new currency, it's theoretically *impossible* –

ALICE. All right, whatever, so people will pay cash. Or – hey! They can bring their kids! We can do a kiddie table in the kitchen, how's that? More fun anyway. Now, how much wine should we get? Do you think people will want red or white?

DIANA. *(As Doug.)* Do you know how embarrassing this is? These are my colleagues! This is a model *I designed* and now it's crashing! This is like kindergarten stuff, this is Econ 101 and I look like a total idiot! There's no way the tenure committee doesn't hear about this!

ALICE. Should I have told him?

I mean, I wasn't even 100 percent sure it was my fault. Could I have really made enough bogus shares to screw up his whole system? I'd made maybe ten or fifteen for Diana, and a bunch for myself, and yeah I guess there had been a few times I didn't tell you about when I stamped out a few here and there as favors for other people who might have mentioned they were short, or... OK, yes, it was definitely all my fault, and he was bound to figure it out eventually.

So I just confessed. I mean, I'm not a sociopath.

Look, it was me, OK? I used your stamp and made the extra shares, I'm really sorry. So, what should we do for dessert, should I just make a pan of brownies, or...

I'm not sure how to describe what happened next.

DIANA. She'd come to my house immediately afterward in, I suppose, a sort of state of shock. She was quiet. She'd brought Holly and we sent the girls to play. She told me about the co-op business, then descended into incoherence.

ALICE. I should have *known*. It was so *obvious*, God! I'm an idiot. Diana. What should I do? I don't know what to –

DIANA. What *is* it, Alice? You're not making sense.

ALICE. I was babbling, I could barely get the words out.

DIANA. She was so pale and shaken at first I feared the worst.

Did he...*strike* you?

ALICE. What? No. God, no. Doug?

I mean yeah he was super upset, I guess you could say he was kind of panicking about his career and everything, he was convinced that this would sink him with his colleagues, that he'd become a laughingstock, but that just seemed ridiculous to me –

(To **DIANA** *as Doug.)* I mean, come on, Doug, they're not going to pass you over for tenure because you fucked up a babysitting co-op!

DIANA. *(As Doug.) You* fucked up the babysitting co-op!

ALICE. Whatever, fine, Doug – Or, yes! *I* fucked it up, so they can't blame you, right?

DIANA. *(As Doug.)* You don't understand, Alice. I can't do this anymore.

ALICE. This, what? Teaching? I don't care about that. I'd be glad. I hate academia.

DIANA. *(As Doug.)* No, this. Us.

ALICE. Us?

The *marriage*?

DIANA. *(As Doug.)* Yes.

ALICE. And he started to tear up again, like he had before, but it was worse this time, much worse, all of a sudden he was *sobbing*, and choking when he tried to get the words out...

DIANA. So that I don't have to enact the histrionics, which I would no doubt do badly, I'll just summarize for you what Alice told me her husband told her.

The major issue was not the counterfeited shares, or Doug's work troubles real or imagined. No. This was merely the trigger for an anguished outpouring over the state of the marriage generally.

You see, the little vacation – the family getaway which for Alice had been so restorative – had been *determinative* for Doug, he said, and not in a good way. It confirmed for him that he could not go on living the quote "absurd farce" their marriage had become.

By now Alice, in relating this to me, was weeping steadily herself: admitting that there *had* been something off about the little vacation, the Sandusky trip, and not just in retrospect: she knew it at the time. That though they did talk and laugh and "relax" together that weekend, whatever ease they'd managed to contrive was through, and ultimately for, Holly. That a hand grasped during a sunset walk on the beach was inevitably too quickly released; that, finally, there was no giggly, furtive delight, only haste and a sense of obligation, in the silent motel room lovemaking while the child slept.

And it wasn't that Doug was in *love* with the student he'd hired to paint their house that summer. Or *knew* that he – or "that" – was what he "really" wanted – in fact he was sure that it wasn't about Merle at all, he actually couldn't wait for him to be done and gone, for it to all be *over*, (*Christ*), it made him sick to think about it now: the tension, the insanity, the – he used the word again – *farce* of the student's frantic visits upstairs to him in his study while Alice sunbathed in the yard below, the guilt and the fear of it all – not that most of these visits were about sex or anything physical, of course not, they weren't *that* dumb or reckless, most were just anguished cut-short discussions about *what the hell were they doing?* Or sudden declarations of devotion, or quickly withdrawn threats of exposure, or just ugly stupid little quarrels of the kind all lovers have.

ALICE. How could I not have seen it?

DIANA. I didn't see it either.

6.

ALICE. That night she fed us. The four of us sat on her back porch and ate a salad she just threw together out of whatever was in her fridge, only because it was Diana it was *excellent.* And we drank a good bottle of wine she had.

The girls played until it got dark. This is late August, so maybe nine or nine-thirty. And then Diana found them some old jars and punched holes in the tin tops and the girls ran around collecting fireflies in the grass. They asked when they had to go to bed.

DIANA. No bedtime! You're on your own recognizance.

ALICE. They asked what that meant.

DIANA. It's Liberty Hall, girls! You can stay up all night if you want! Run riot! Cry Havoc, and let slip the dogs of war! RAGE AGAINST THE DYING OF THE LIGHT AND LET THE WILD RUMPUS START! You can even...*use my art supplies.*

ALICE. They looked a little freaked out then, and retreated into the yard with their jars.

DIANA. Look at them out there.

ALICE. Yes.

DIANA. God they are beautiful.

ALICE. Yep.

> *(Beat.)*

DIANA. There's something I need to ask you. I don't want you to be upset.

ALICE. Okay.

DIANA. Do you have any more of Merle's weed?

*(**ALICE** digs in her bag. Finds a battered joint. Gives it to **DIANA**. **DIANA** lights it, drags.)*

ALICE. Better enjoy it. No more where that came from.

*(**DIANA** hands it to **ALICE**, who waves it off.)*

DIANA. You're not going to?

ALICE. I don't feel like it.

*(**DIANA** smokes alone.)*

Can I ask *you* something?

DIANA. Yes.

ALICE. Is it true you're an adjunct?

DIANA. What do you mean?

ALICE. I mean, I thought you were an art professor. I mean, you are an art professor, right?

DIANA. At present I teach part-time at the University. Continuing ed. Retirees, mostly. I have no degree.

ALICE. God, I always thought...

DIANA. Yes, I know.

I could never quite finish it. The Magnum Opus. The – literal – "masterpiece." My art school friends would say to me, "For Chrissake, just give them something, what is the matter with you?" They were right. "It's an MFA thesis project! They'll take anything! Stick a dildo in a fondue pot and sign it and you're *done*."

Does it matter to you?

ALICE. What?

DIANA. That I'm a failure.

ALICE. Come on. You're not.

DIANA. Of course I am. Do you think I wanted to be a part-time art instructor in Columbus, Ohio? Great things were promised me, Alice. I promised them to myself. How could anyone so *uncompromising* not be bound for the New York galleries? Maybe an international career. London or Berlin.

I can simply never finish the work. To my own satisfaction, let alone anyone else's. It's a pity, isn't it?

I've even thought quite seriously of quitting.

ALICE. Why?

DIANA. I've left enough incomplete. Why add to the pile?

ALICE. Stop it. You can't quit. You're *good*.

DIANA. Thank you. But you don't, and I mean this with the greatest respect, really know what you're talking about.

ALICE. You're not a fucking failure, all right?

I mean if you are, God, what does that make me? I don't even know where we're supposed to sleep tonight!

DIANA. Here. You'll stay here as long as you like.

ALICE. But what am I going to *do*?

DIANA. I don't understand. Do you mean, in *life*?

ALICE. Yes, in my life! I don't know *anything*. I don't know who I am. I don't want to lose my family but maybe it's already gone. I don't know what I'm going to do next week, next month, *tomorrow morning – Tell me what I'm supposed to do.*

DIANA. Are you sure you want that?

ALICE. Yes.

DIANA. When I've done it before you haven't liked it.

ALICE. This isn't like before.

DIANA. All right. You should do the only thing you can.

Start over. Start fresh.

Take the opportunity that's been given to you, Alice. That very few of us are ever given. Leave behind everything that's caused you to squander yourself. And become something completely *new*.

ALICE. I can't just...*do* that.

DIANA. You absolutely can.

ALICE. What about my marriage?

DIANA. You are not your marriage. You don't need it.

ALICE. That's easy for you to say. You don't need *anyone*.

(*Beat.*)

DIANA. Is that what you think?

ALICE. Yes.

DIANA. Then you really don't know me at all.

(*Beat.*)

ALICE. Sorry.

DIANA. No. I'm not entirely myself.

ALICE. Me either. I think I need to go to sleep.

DIANA. I'll make up the sofa for you. The girls can sleep in Gretchen's room.

ALICE. Is it okay if I just stay out here? I'm too tired to move.

DIANA. All right.

ALICE. Diana?

DIANA. Yes?

ALICE. Make sure Holly brushes her teeth?

I woke up very early. The rising sun woke me. I'd slept very hard. I was disoriented for a minute. Then I remembered everything.

I pulled the blanket that Diana must have put on me over my head against the sun and just *cowered* for, I don't know, ten minutes maybe, until it got too hot and I *had* to get up.

DIANA. She was gone when I awoke. She and Holly. She'd done the dishes from the night before, folded the blanket.

I assumed she'd gone home. I called her that night but there was no answer.

I called the next day and she *did* pick up.

Alice? It's me, it's Diana.

ALICE. Hey, I can't really talk right now.

DIANA. I'm concerned. Are you all right?

ALICE. Yeah.

DIANA. Her voice sounded strained – possibly Doug was in the room – but brisk too.

ALICE. Look, thanks for the other night.

DIANA. Of course. Is there anything else I can –

ALICE. No. Thanks Diana. I'll call you in a couple days, OK?

DIANA. Alice, if you need somewhere to go –

But she'd hung up.

I went into my studio. The canvases stacked three deep against the walls.

I looked around the rest of my house.

My God how I hated it. Every stick of furniture. The cabinets of crockery. Every book on every shelf: every title, every spine. The objects I'd selected to *intersperse* with the books: how *unusual*, what an *eye* you have! What a pathetically over-embroidered shroud I'd weaved to drape over my lifeless life.

I knew at once what I must do.

What *Alice* and I must do.

Gretchen and Holly and Alice and I.

ALICE. She comes to the house. Gretchen in the back seat. Her car is packed. A U-haul trailer hitched to the back.

DIANA. We're leaving.

ALICE. What? I don't understand.

DIANA. I'm leaving Columbus. I've sold my house and most of my possessions. Everything I own is now in that U-haul. Do you want to come with me or not?

ALICE. Where would we go?

DIANA. Wherever we want. To be determined.

ALICE. Now?

DIANA. Yes. Right now.

ALICE. I can't just go away with you!

DIANA. You absolutely can.

ALICE. I pack two suitcases, one for me, one for Holly. Oh, and bring one other thing.

Doug protests, hysterically, but we're already out the door, and into Diana's car.

DIANA. We drive.

ALICE. We drive all night. Mostly I drive. I'm a better driver.

DIANA. And six more nights.

ALICE. We're driving across the Country!

DIANA. Chicago. Cedar Rapids.

ALICE. Des Moines. Omaha.

DIANA. The Great Plains! We're seeing America!

ALICE. America! In the summer of 1976!

DIANA. Across Nebraska. Cheyenne, Wyoming.

ALICE. Salt Lake City.

DIANA. Reno! Carson City.

ALICE. Sacramento.

DIANA. There's no need to mention Sacramento.

ALICE. Part of the journey.

DIANA. And finally…San Francisco.

ALICE. San Francisco!

DIANA. Where we found a coldwater flat in a hard-done-by but vibrant and striving district of this then most bohemian and exhilarating of American cities.

And began to shape a life: these two mothers with their two daughters.

Mine is built of course around my art, which, spurred by Alice's encouragement and the freshness of our changed circumstances I attack with a renewed, confident vigor and sense of purpose, soon endorsed, to my delight and astonishment, by the offer of a local gallery show.

Several pieces sell, which leads in less time than I could have imagined to my being taken up by a dealer with a gallery in New York City. Commissions follow, and acquisitions by some smaller contemporary art museums. I am, in a limited but real sense, "known." My bank account now holds money I'd earned myself.

Gretchen grows alongside her close friend and quasi-sister Holly. Two beautiful young women, growing up, growing wise, making their mothers almost insanely proud.

Alice in time discovers her own vocation. The inveterate paperback reader discovers she's a writer! Sitting up late at night after the girls have gone to sleep at "the" desk – the one I'd picked out for her, the *one item* she'd salvaged from her former life in Columbus – she begins scratching out sketches and stories – blunt, funny, disarming – like her – which, after some friendly but *firm* editorial input from me, she stitches into a novel-length narrative which becomes a bestselling book in the waning months of the 1970s, later made into a memorable, if minor, film.

And so we live on, two friends, two mothers, two artists, entwined in each others' lives and the lives of our children, our successes and sorrows inextricable too, and owing to a friendship which sustains and challenges us in equal measure as the years, and then the decades, march on.

It's marvelous, isn't it?

ALICE. It is. It really is.

DIANA. Of course none of that happened.

  (Beat.)

Alice, it's Diana.

ALICE. Hey, I can't really talk right now.

DIANA. I'm concerned. Are you all right?

ALICE. Yeah. Hey, thanks for the other night.

DIANA. Of course. Is there anything else I can –

ALICE. No. Thanks Diana. I'll call you in a couple days, OK?

DIANA. Alice, if you need somewhere to go –

ALICE. I had to hang up.

DIANA. Alice, if you need *anything* –

She hung up.

ALICE. Doug was sitting right there, and honestly I was worried about him at the moment: ever since I'd gotten home after the night at Diana's he was sick, like, literally sick with regret and agony and he couldn't eat, could barely talk, all he could do was hold my hand and beg me to forgive him.

I mean, "forgive?" It wasn't even so much about that as it was more, like, Well, what the fuck are we going to do now? I mean, what does he want, does he know? Does he even want me anymore? Do I want him? And what's best for Holly, and, I mean, everything, Jesus! I mean "forgiveness" is sort of the least of our problems, right?

He agreed with that. He agreed we had a lot to figure out. We had *everything* to figure out and he said we should go into therapy and that seemed like, Yeah, we need to do that. And man, this was going to be a long haul, this was going to be hard no matter what. Plus he still had to finish his work and get tenure (which he did, incidentally), plus the school year was starting up and Holly and I had to deal with all that, new clothes and a new backpack and all the stuff that's life-or-death to a kid.

So it was a while before I got back to Diana.

After I finally did we had dinner together once a week or so for a while. It wasn't quite the same as before. She seemed, I don't know, a little preoccupied. God knows I was. She talked a couple times about maybe moving. I think she mentioned San Francisco, which seemed sort of random; she also mentioned New York I think? Finding a cheap place, doing the whole sort of bohemian thing. She even said I should go with her once. Kind of as a joke. At least I think it was a joke. But she never brought it up again.

Through the winter and into 1977 we didn't see each other so much. Doug and I were deep, *deep* into the whole saving-the-marriage thing. Only I'd realized, duh, it *wasn't* a saving-the-marriage thing, it was an Am I happy? thing. Diana was right about that. Jesus, had she been right.

The divorce went through in '78.

That same fall Diana got a new job, at Kenyon College.

We visited a few times, me and Holly. Diana had an even more gorgeous house there, and now she was full-time: a move up, not teaching anymore, some kind of administrative thing. I think she was pleased about that, though of course she wouldn't let on. I did get the impression she was lonely. I don't think she had a lot of friends there. She didn't have many friends at Ohio State and it must have been hard coming into a much much smaller place.

Kenyon isn't that far away from Columbus, less than two hours, but you know how it is. The visits got less frequent, and as the girls got older inevitably they didn't have as much in common. They were pen-pals for a while but of course that dropped off.

I got a teaching certificate. Middle school English. Other teachers will tell you middle school kids are the worst, but I don't know, I like them, they're so crazy and fucked up at that age, it's interesting to try to figure them out, and they're fun, teaching them and reading books with them is fun.

There were men too of course. Some shorter term, some longer. Some nice, some not so much. We don't have to get into all that.

DIANA. Years went by.

ALICE. Diana sent out cards at the holidays and she always sent me one. She designed the cards herself, they were really beautiful, really meticulous and austere. Not great *holiday* cards actually, but little works of art all the same. I don't send anything, I'm not a card person.

After a decade or so the cards stopped. Maybe I fell off her list.

I wasn't offended or anything. It's not like I had made an effort to be in touch. Sure, I felt guilty about that. I thought about writing or emailing – I even found her email online at the Kenyon Art Department – but so much time had passed it seemed weirder, I don't know, embarrassing somehow to try. You know how it is. You just feel sort of passive and resentful of the thing you know you should have done but didn't, you forget about it for long stretches, until finally on the rare occasions when you do think of it you're just like, well, unfortunately *that's* not ever going to happen.

Then, one day – today – holy shit. I saw her in New York.

7.

DIANA. Alice.

ALICE. Oh my God.

What are you doing here? I mean, the show, duh, but –
Oh my God.

(They embrace.)

DIANA. How are you?

ALICE. I'm good. Do you…live here now, or –

DIANA. Oh no, no. I just flew in for this.

ALICE. Oh! Sure.

DIANA. How did you happen to hear about it?

ALICE. I didn't. I was just walking by the museum and I
saw the banner and I was like, Wow, I've got to –

DIANA. Yes.

ALICE. It's really something.

DIANA. Yes. They did a nice job.

ALICE. It's so crowded!

DIANA. Well, it's been hyped quite a bit. Overhyped, I
should say. "The first complete retrospective." It's not
quite true of course. In North America, yes.

ALICE. Right.

DIANA. Do you live in New York?

ALICE. No, no, I'm just visiting Holly.

DIANA. What is she doing here?

ALICE. Med school.

DIANA. Really. That's wonderful.

ALICE. She's doing her residency. She took a few years off to have a baby but now she's nearly done.

DIANA. You're a grandmother.

ALICE. Ugh, God. Yes. I mean it's great, I love it. I love him. I just have a *lot* of trouble thinking of myself that way. It's been almost two years and I'm still not used to it: "Grandma…"

DIANA. Of course. Of course.

ALICE. How is Gretchen?

DIANA. She's…

ALICE. Wait. This is stupid. Just standing here. Do you want to go to the cafe and get a cup of coffee or something? I've seen the show, basically. I mean, I don't want to interrupt your experience or anything –

DIANA. Not at all. Let's get a cup of coffee.

ALICE. It really was just luck I'd gone in. I had an hour to kill before I had to pick up Nicholas from his morning daycare – you don't have to *send* him to daycare this morning, I'm in town for God's sake, let me have him! I'd practically *screamed* at my daughter, but Holly didn't want to interrupt his "routine," she's very into "routine," I guess it's a thing now – Anyway. I saw the banner with the title of the show. I don't even know if I clocked the teeny connection to Diana, maybe I did subconsciously, because I went in.

DIANA. I'd made a point to be in New York for the first week of the 2003 MoMA Paul Klee retrospective. I'd made my peace with Klee and the influence he'd had on my unfathomably distant younger self. I'd even written a short monograph on him for the small online journal published by the Kenyon College Art Department. Very few people read it, but I was pleased with it.

ALICE. It was one of those stupid, huge, really crowded shows where you can barely see the art 'cause of all the people, so I just sort of made a quick circuit of the rooms and was on my way out when I heard someone say my name.

DIANA. Alice.

ALICE. I knew it was her before I turned around.

(At a table:)

I'm so sorry but I only have a few minutes. I have to pick up my grandson at one o'clock.

DIANA. It's all right.

ALICE. I'd call but they're so strict about pick-up times, it's crazy.

DIANA. I completely understand. It's just good to see you.

ALICE. It's good to see you too.

(Beat.)

But hey! I'm not going home until the day after tomorrow, maybe we could meet for breakfast, or –

DIANA. I have a four o'clock flight this afternoon I'm afraid.

ALICE. Oh.

DIANA. I'm taking a cab straight to the airport from here.

ALICE. Oh, that's too bad.

DIANA. Yes.

(Beat.)

ALICE. I'm just embarrassed I haven't been in touch.

DIANA. Don't be. I wasn't much better.

ALICE. I loved those cards.

DIANA. Thank you.

ALICE. People must have been crazy for them. Why did you stop sending them out?

DIANA. I suppose I just got tired of making them.

ALICE. They were really beautiful. I hope you're making something else.

DIANA. I put most of my energy into the Department these days, committee work, there's no end to it.

ALICE. I bet.

(Beat.)

You look great by the way.

DIANA. I was going to say the same to you.

ALICE. Aw.

DIANA. But then I remembered how much I hate when people say that.

ALICE. I hate it too! "You look great…"

DIANA. *"Considering…"*

ALICE. Considering the *mileage…*

DIANA. Exactly. Yes.

(Beat.)

ALICE. Diana.

DIANA. Yes.

ALICE. You haven't said. How is Gretchen?

DIANA. She's…had a bit of a rough patch.

ALICE. Oh.

DIANA. But things are much better now.

ALICE. That's great.

You'll tell her we say Hi? Me and Holly both.

DIANA. Of course I will. Thank you.

> *(Beat.)*

ALICE. Oh, shit. I hate to say it but –

DIANA. You have to go.

ALICE. Yes. I'm really sorry –

DIANA. No, please. I should go too. I always like to get to the airport early. It's a bit neurotic.

ALICE. No, it makes total sense.

DIANA. We paid for the coffees.

ALICE. I promised this time I would stay in touch. We exchanged contact information like you do, tapped it into our phones, tic tic tic.

DIANA. When we said goodbye outside the museum something happened.

ALICE. I suddenly found myself with tears in my eyes, hugging her quite hard and saying how much I missed her.

> **(ALICE** *suddenly embraces* **DIANA**, *hugging her tightly. It lasts a moment, then they move apart.)*

I swear I hadn't meant to do it. But it's how I felt.

DIANA. The hug, yes.

I was surprised. And I suppose still disconcerted by her mention of "cards." I had not sent out "cards," I had sent out *a* card, annually, to her. In fairness, there was no way she could have known this.

And by her asking about Gretchen, inevitable as it was. And by the failure of my usual euphemism of choice, "She's had a bit of a rough patch," to appear as dependably as accustomed. I nearly submitted a blunter accounting: Gretchen's move back in with me;

the countless failed relationships; the substance abuse; what I strongly suspect was a suicide attempt two years ago.

I said none of this. What would it accomplish?

I saw Alice make the decision not to press. Did I catch a flicker of pity? I didn't begrudge her her happiness, I didn't want pity in return.

ALICE. I told her I'd wait with her while she got a taxi.

Oof, mistake. It took a few minutes and *that* was awkward. Has that ever happened to you? The big emotional goodbye, embrace, so wonderful to see you!, all that stuff, but then something happens and you can't actually *go*, you have to stand there together for a few minutes: it's this weird moment of limbo and there's nothing left to say?

(Beat. Sounds of traffic.)

There's a cab.

DIANA. Finally…

ALICE. I watched her get in and pull away. I thought about her waiting for my bus on Sixth Avenue, and on the long ride uptown to the daycare to pick up Nicholas.

I was so glad to see him.

DIANA. Do I miss Alice?

I'm not sure. I'm not sure if I miss the person or the memory of those few months in 1976.

It was such a short period of time. We hardly knew each other, really. And we were so different. We were really only brought together by the children.

It's not at all a surprise that we didn't stay close.

Curtain